Bogeymen Don't
Play Football

There are more books about the Bailey School Kids!
Have you read these adventures?

Bogeymen Don't Play Football

by Debbie Dadey
and
Marcia Thornton Jones

illustrated by John Steven Gurney

A
LITTLE APPLE
PAPERBACK

SCHOLASTIC INC.
New York   Toronto   London   Auckland   Sydney

To Steve Jones and his boogie-woogie basement band. — MTJ

In memory of Arthur F. Bailey — D.D.

No part of this publication may be reproduced in whole or in part, or stored in a retrieval system, or transmitted in any form or by any means, electronic, mechanical, photocopying, recording, or otherwise, without written permission of the publisher. For information regarding permission, write to Scholastic Inc., Attention: Permissions Department, 555 Broadway, New York, NY 10012.

ISBN 0-590-25701-3

10 9 8 7 6 5 4 3 2 1   7 8 9/9 0 1/0 2/0

Printed in the U.S.A.   40

First Scholastic printing, August 1997

Book design by Laurie Williams

Contents

1

Mr. Bogey

"Did you hear the news?" Liza asked Eddie, Melody, and Howie. The four friends stood under the oak tree waiting for the morning bell to ring.

"What news?" Eddie asked. "Did the zookeepers change their minds? Are they putting you in a cage?"

Liza frowned at Eddie. "No," she said. "For your information, we are getting a new teacher."

Eddie jumped up in the air and cheered. "All right! We're getting rid of Mrs. Jeepers." Mrs. Jeepers was their third-grade teacher. She was so strict she made a drill sergeant seem like a kitty cat. The fact that she lived in a haunted house and spoke with a strange Romanian accent made most kids believe she was a vampire.

"Wait a minute," Melody said, grabbing Eddie's arm. "Don't get so excited. We're getting a student teacher. We'll still have Mrs. Jeepers for our real teacher."

Eddie looked like a popped balloon. "How could you get my hopes up like that?" he asked Liza.

Howie patted Eddie on the back. "I'm sure this new student teacher will be very nice."

"I doubt it," Eddie said. "Any student teacher of Mrs. Jeepers' has to be weird."

The bell rang before Howie could argue, and the four kids trudged into their classroom. Eddie put a new pencil inside his desk. When he looked up he saw black, black, and more black.

The man standing in front of Eddie wasn't just tall. His shoulders were as wide as three school desks pushed to-gether, and his neck was so huge his shirt wouldn't button. He wore a black

2

shirt, black tie, and black pants. He even had a black earring in one ear. The man took one look at Eddie and frowned.

"Hi," Eddie said in a squeaky voice.

"No talking," the man bellowed. "I am Mr. Bogey, your new student teacher. We'll have no goofing off. Get out a book and start reading. You have a report due tomorrow."

Eddie grabbed a book from his desk. He peeked over the top of the book as Mr. Bogey walked around the room. Their regular teacher, Mrs. Jeepers, was nowhere to be seen. All the kids in the classroom were already reading silently.

"Pssst," Eddie hissed at Howie. "What's wrong with this guy?"

Howie shrugged. "Be quiet," Howie warned.

But it was too late. Mr. Bogey appeared beside Eddie's desk and pointed a huge finger at Eddie. "You'd better watch out," Mr. Bogey told him. "I'll have to get you if you don't do your work."

Mr. Bogey had so many muscles in his arms, Eddie figured it would be a snap for Mr. Bogey to twirl him around on his pinky and toss him headfirst into the Dumpster. But that didn't bother Eddie. After all, student teachers weren't real teachers. Eddie glanced at the book on his desk. It was about airplanes. Eddie didn't feel like reading about airplanes, but he did feel like making paper ones.

Eddie slammed his book closed and ripped paper from his notebook. Then he started folding. Eddie was so busy folding super-duper paper planes, he didn't notice Mr. Bogey watching him. And Mr. Bogey was frowning.

2

Watch Out!

"What's wrong with you?" Liza asked Eddie the next morning.

Eddie dragged his feet across the playground. His friends were waiting for him in their favorite meeting place under the oak tree. When Eddie reached his friends, he dropped his bookbag so he could rub his eyes.

"You look like you were up all night," Melody said.

Eddie yawned. "I was," he admitted.

"Why?" Howie asked. "Were you up doing your math homework?"

Eddie shook his head.

"Did you write your book report?" Melody asked.

"What book report?" Eddie asked.

"The report Mr. Bogey told us about," Howie told his friend.

"Eddie wouldn't stay up to do homework," Liza said. "Something else must have kept him up."

Eddie nodded. "That something was under my bed. It kept going *THUMP, THUMP, THUMP.* It was awful."

Melody smiled. "Maybe it was a monster."

"Or the bogeyman," Liza said with a giggle.

Eddie rolled his eyes. "There is no such thing as a bogeyman."

"Nobody knows that for sure," Howie said.

"I do," Eddie said. "Because I looked under my bed."

Liza's eyes were big. She always ran and jumped into her bed just in case something was hiding underneath, but she never actually looked under her bed. She was too afraid something would be

9

looking back at her. "What did you find?" she asked.

"Diamond!" Eddie sputtered. Diamond was his aunt Mathilda's dalmatian.

"How did your aunt's dog get under your bed?" Melody asked.

Eddie shook his head. "I have no idea. Aunt Mathilda said she didn't let him out. But there he was, beating his tail against the floor right under my bed. I didn't get any sleep."

Melody patted Eddie on the shoulder. "Well, I have some news that will make you feel better," she said. Then she waved five green slips of paper under his nose.

"What's that?" Eddie asked as he grabbed for them.

Melody snatched them away as a girl named Carey walked up beside her. "They're tickets," Melody said. "Bailey Bomber tickets!"

"My dad says the new Bailey City football team is so good they should be a

professional team," Carey said. "He has tickets for all the games."

"Well, my dad got tickets for this week-end," Melody bragged. "And he said I could take my three best friends."

"All right!" Eddie cheered. "Now, all we have to do is survive the rest of the week."

"And Mr. Bogey," Liza added.

"Mr. Bogey doesn't scare me," Eddie said.

"No," Melody giggled, "but a puppy dog under your bed does."

"Very funny, dog breath," Eddie snapped.

"You better watch out," Howie warned. "Mr. Bogey said he'd get you if you didn't do your work."

"I didn't do my homework," Eddie admitted.

"Me, neither," Carey said. "But I'm not worried. After all, Mr. Bogey is just a student teacher."

"Maybe," Howie said. "But I have a feeling we all better watch out."

3

The Game

"Go, Bombers!" Eddie screamed. Howie, Liza, and Melody yelled, too. Some of the football players turned around to wave. The Saturday game was just beginning, and the four friends were sitting in the bleachers right behind the Bailey Bombers. The team looked great in their new black uniforms. Even their black helmets sparkled in the afternoon sun.

"I feel like I'm sitting with the team," Liza said. "We'll be able to see every move they make."

"These seats are great!" Howie told Melody.

"They're even better than Carey's," Eddie said with a grin. Carey sat right behind Eddie.

"I heard that," Carey said. Eddie turned around and gave Carey his most innocent smile. Then he tried to untie Carey's shoes.

"I'm lucky I got to come," Carey said. "My dad is still cleaning up my room."

"What happened?" Eddie asked. "Did you spill your ugly potion?"

"Very funny," Carey said.

"What happened?" Liza asked.

"It happened the other night," Carey told them. "I was supposed to be doing

my homework, but I was writing in my diary instead. There was a strange *THUMP, THUMP, THUMP* from under my bed."

"This is just what happened to Eddie," Howie said softly. But the football crowd started to cheer, and his friends didn't hear him.

"And then," Carey continued after the cheering stopped, "there was a big *whoosh*, and water squirted everywhere. Dad said a water pipe broke."

"Shhh," Melody warned. "The game started. We have to watch. The Bailey Bombers move fast!"

The Bomber running back darted down the field with the football. The other team looked like they were running in slow motion. When the running back crossed the goal line, everybody stood up and cheered.

"I bet he's the fastest runner in the world," Howie said with a sigh. "I hope I can play that well when I get older."

"Dream on," Melody said. "That guy moves like he's trying to outrun the sun."

The four friends watched the Bomber running back jog toward the sidelines for a drink. Before he grabbed the water bottle, the Bailey Bomber pulled off his helmet.

Then he turned and frowned right at the Bailey School kids.

"Oh, no," Liza squealed. "Look who it is!"

4

Crazy Day Job

"Why would the star player of the Bailey Bombers want to be a teacher?" Howie asked.

"I know the answer to that," Eddie said. "He's crazy. Why else would anyone want to be a teacher and spend the rest of his life in school?"

Liza punched Eddie's arm. "Mr. Bogey is not crazy," she said. "He just needs a day job. Football players don't make much money."

"They do if they're professional players," Carey said.

Melody pointed to the players dressed in black. "He should be a pro player," she said. "He definitely knows what he's doing."

The Bailey Bombers were lining up on

the field. One big burly man slapped Mr. Bogey on the back and yelled, "Let's go!"

The Bailey Bombers were ready. The other team looked tiny next to the big-shouldered Bombers.

"That other team might as well pack it up and go home," Eddie said. "The Bombers are going to win this game."

"It's not over until it's over," Melody said.

"This game was over before it even started," Eddie bragged. "Bailey City

might not have much, but this year we have a great football team. It's about time we got something good."

When Mr. Bogey recovered a fumble, everyone in the Bailey City stands cheered. "Mr. Bogey might be an odd student teacher," Melody said after the cheering died down, "but he's a fantastic football player."

"Odd isn't the word for him," Carey said. "He's freaky. He acts like he's going to bite your head off if you don't have your homework right away."

"He can't be too normal," Howie agreed. "After all, he gets along with Mrs. Jeepers, and we all know Mrs. Jeepers is definitely not a normal teacher." The kids nodded. Every one of them feared the worst about their teacher. They thought the strange brooch she wore gave her special powers.

"We're doomed," Carey said sadly.

"Maybe in school," Eddie said. "But

this is football, and school is a million years away."

"It's the day after tomorrow," Liza reminded him. "But I'm sure we'll be fine as long as we do our homework."

"Who has time for homework?" Eddie yelled as the crowd cheered again. Mr. Bogey was running toward the Bombers' end zone. He crossed the line and made a touchdown!

"All right!" Eddie cheered. He was so busy yelling he didn't notice that Mr. Bogey was staring right at him.

5

Heads Up

Melody threw her football at Eddie. It was Monday morning, and Eddie was walking across the playground with a boy named Huey. Liza and Howie waited under the oak tree with Melody. The football arched high over the playground and then spiraled straight at Eddie.

"Heads up!" Howie yelled to Eddie, but Howie was too late. The football thumped Eddie in the chest. Eddie stumbled and sat down hard on the ground. Melody's football rolled past Huey's feet.

"I'm so fast, Eddie didn't even see me," Melody cheered from under the oak tree. "Bailey Bombers, sign me up! I'm ready to play!"

"You're not that fast," Eddie snapped.

"Ah-choo!" Huey sneezed and then reached out to help Eddie up.

Eddie wiped off the seat of his pants. "I would've caught it if I wasn't half asleep," Eddie said.

"How can you be tired?" Howie asked. "We had the whole weekend to do our homework and rest."

"I was too busy watching the Bailey Bombers," Eddie said.

"Me, too," Huey admitted. Then he sneezed again.

"And I didn't get any sleep because every time I turned out the lights," Eddie continued, "it sounded like there was a party going on under my bed."

"Is your aunt's dog still sleeping under your bed?" Howie asked. "I thought you took Diamond back to your aunt's house."

"I did," Eddie said. "But I still keep hearing noises."

"Did it sound like someone scrap-ing long fingernails on the wall?" Huey asked, his face as white as the stitching on Melody's football. "Did you hear thumps that sounded like somebody's head being bounced on the floor?"

"I think that cold has gone to your head," Melody said to Huey. "And snot has taken over your brains."

Howie and Liza giggled, but Eddie wasn't laughing. "Is this some kind of joke?" Eddie sputtered. "Did you have something to do with those noises?"

Huey stepped back until his shoulders rested against the oak tree. "Of course not," he said.

"Then how did you know about the noises I heard?" Eddie demanded.

"Because," Huey said, "it sounds like something is under my bed, too."

Melody laughed out loud. "Nothing could fit under your bed with all the junk you keep there!" Everyone knew about Huey's messy room.

"That's what my mom said," Huey admitted. "She made me clean under my bed. There were enough dust bunnies to wipe out every kid in Bailey City with allergies. I haven't stopped sneezing since yesterday. But I found more than dust."

"Did you find some lost toys?" Melody asked.

Huey nodded. "There were some old things. And most of them belonged to me. But not all of them."

"What are you talking about?" Eddie asked.

"There were cookie crumbs and a soda can," Huey said in a whisper.

Eddie poked Huey in his stomach. "It sounds like you've had too many late-night snacks," he told Huey.

"Those cookies weren't mine," Huey said. "I think someone — or some-*thing* — has been living under my bed!"

Liza giggled and Melody laughed out loud. "Don't tell me you believe in monsters under your bed," Melody said.

"Melody is right," Howie said. "You're always munching on something. You probably just forgot you took those cookies to your room."

"Maybe," Huey said, reaching deep into his backpack. "But then how do you explain this?"

6

Who's Under the Bed?

"Wow!" Melody whispered like she just met Troy Aikman. "Where did you get this?" She gently took the ball from Huey and read the name signed on the bumpy leather. "This football was signed by the Bailey Bombers' coach," she said.

"How did you end up with that?" Liza asked.

"I told you," Huey said. "I found it under my bed."

"Well, if you didn't put it there, who did?" Eddie asked.

Liza giggled. "Maybe the bogeyman did it."

Melody laughed and Eddie rolled his eyes. But Howie grabbed Liza's arm. He started breathing really hard.

"What's wrong?" Liza asked.

Howie held his throat and tried to talk.

Eddie grabbed Howie around the chest. "We'd better do that Hamlick thingee before he dies."

Howie jerked away from Eddie. "It's the Heimlich maneuver," Howie told Eddie. "But it's not necessary."

"You looked like you swallowed a dinosaur bone," Eddie pointed out.

Howie shook his head. "I'm not choking," he said. "I just had an awful idea."

Eddie shook his finger in front of Howie's nose. "How many times do I have to tell you," he said. "Thinking is dangerous!"

"Not as dangerous as our student teacher," Howie said.

"What does Mr. Bogey have to do with cookies and a football under Huey's bed?" Melody asked.

Howie swallowed and looked around the playground to make sure no one else was listening. "Because," he finally said, "Mr. Bogey is the bogeyman!"

Eddie laughed and slapped Howie on the back. "That's a good one," he said. "My grandmother always said the bogeyman would get me if I didn't watch out. She likes to kid around, too."

"I'm not joking," Howie told his friend. "The bogeyman has moved to Bailey City, and he's a Bailey Bomber."

"And I'm the Super Bowl player of the year," Melody giggled.

"What would the bogeyman be doing in Bailey City?" Liza asked.

"I don't know," Howie told them. "But it all adds up. The bogeyman hides out under beds, and he keeps kids up with terrible noises. That's exactly what's been happening to Eddie ever since Mr. Bogey showed up in our classroom."

"He did say he was going to get Eddie," Liza said.

"All teachers say that about Eddie," Melody said. "That doesn't prove any-thing."

"But this does." Howie pointed to the

Bailey Bombers' football that Melody held. "Whenever you look under the bed for the bogeyman, he disappears. Only this time, the bogeyman left one of his toys under Huey's bed."

"Are you telling me the bogeyman is living under my bed?" Huey squeaked.

Howie nodded. "But don't worry, now that you cleaned under your bed he'll probably move into your closet."

Huey looked like he was ready to faint.

"Don't listen to Howie," Melody said. "I'm pretty sure the bogeyman doesn't play football."

"Melody's right," Eddie said. Then he grinned and grabbed the Bailey Bomber football from Melody. "But we do!"

Eddie tucked the football under his arm and took off running. Melody raced after him. Even Liza, Howie, and Huey joined in the fun. They chased Eddie all around the playground.

Melody was right on his heels. She

reached out to tackle Eddie, but she never got a chance.

Just as Eddie raced past the oak tree, a tall, dark shadow stepped in Eddie's way. Eddie tried to stop, but he tripped on his shoelace and rolled to the ground. Eddie looked up and up and up, right into the face of Mr. Bogey.

"You better watch out," Mr. Bogey said. "Or I'm going to get you!"

7

Bogeyman Boogers

"I thought Eddie was bogeyman boogers," Melody admitted after school. "But all Mr. Bogey made him do was stay after school and do his homework."

"Huey, too," Liza said. Melody, Liza, and Howie waited under the oak tree for their friends.

"I still don't understand how Mr. Bogey sneaked up on us this morning," Liza said. "He's as big as a grizzly bear. How did we miss him?"

"The bogeyman can sneak up on anyone," Howie said softly.

"Don't tell me you still believe that bogeyman baloney," Melody said. "Mr. Bogey is a strict student teacher, but he isn't a monster that lives under beds."

"He does seem to pop up in strange places," Liza said.

"Like under Eddie's and Huey's beds," Howie finished.

"And in your imagination," Melody told her friend.

"Go ahead and joke," Howie said. "But if I were you, I'd do Mr. Bogey's homework."

"What does homework have to do with monsters under my bed?" Melody asked.

"Think about it," Howie said. "Eddie and Huey didn't do their homework. They didn't even try."

"So?" Melody asked. "Carey didn't do her homework, either."

"AHHHH!" Liza screamed. "Howie's right. Mr. Bogey is the bogeyman!"

Melody put her hands on her hips. "Don't tell me you believe in Howie's imaginary monsters," she said.

Liza grabbed Melody's arm. "Don't you get it?" Liza asked. "Carey, Eddie, and Huey heard awful noises under their beds, and they're the ones Mr. Bogey said he would get for not doing their homework!"

"Mr. Bogey meant he was going to get them and make them stay after school," Melody explained.

"If you're so sure," Howie said, "why don't you prove it?"

Melody shook her head so hard her pigtails bopped her on the nose. "I'm not about to spend the night under Howie's bed," she said. "That would give me nightmares for the rest of my life."

"You won't have to," Howie said. "All you have to do is promise not to do your homework."

"But she'll get in trouble," Liza argued.

"It's the only way to prove Mr. Bogey isn't the bogeyman," Howie said. "If he isn't, Melody will sleep like a baby. But if he is, she'll be up all night listening to the bogeyman boogie-woogie under her bed."

"I don't believe in the bogeyman," Melody snapped.

"Then you'll do it?" Howie asked.

But Melody didn't get to answer because a green van pulled up to the curb and honked. As soon as Melody saw her father's van, she raced across the playground and leaned in the window.

"Yahoo!!!" Melody cheered and ran back to her friends. "Dad got us more Bailey Bomber tickets. We're going to the game tonight! We even get to tour the locker room before the game!"

Howie looked very pale. "What's wrong?" Melody asked.

"If we go to the game," Howie said slowly, "we won't have time to do our homework. That means only one thing. The bogeyman is going to get us!"

8

Naked

"Are they naked?" Liza asked, holding her hand over her eyes as she followed Howie, Melody, Eddie, and Melody's dad into the Bailey Bombers' locker room.

Melody pulled Liza's hand away from her eyes. "Don't be silly," Melody told her. "The game is ready to start. Everyone is dressed."

The locker room was crammed with big men in shoulder pads and black uniforms. Liza felt like a tiny ant among huge anteaters. The Bailey Bombers' coach smiled at Melody's dad and shook his hand. "Welcome," the coach said. "Let me introduce you to the team."

The coach took them around to meet every enormous player. When they stopped in front of Mr. Bogey, Liza

gulped. Mr. Bogey had black paint smeared on his cheeks and a frown on his face.

"What are you doing here?" Mr. Bogey asked them.

The coach laughed. "These kids have come to see the best team in town play," he told Mr. Bogey.

"They should be doing their homework," Mr. Bogey growled and pounded one huge fist into the other.

Melody's father patted Melody on her shoulder. "Melody always finishes her homework," he told Mr. Bogey proudly.

Mr. Bogey nodded at Melody's father before looking at Liza, Eddie, Melody, and Howie. "Do your homework, or I'll have to get you," Mr. Bogey warned.

He grabbed his black helmet and set it on his head. Only his black beady eyes showed from behind the face mask.

Melody pretended not to be afraid. "Good luck in the game," she squeaked.

"Let's get moving," the coach yelled. "It's game time."

The Bailey Bombers sounded like a herd of wild buffalo stampeding out of the locker room. Eddie, Melody, Howie, Liza, and Melody's dad followed the team out the door. While the kids settled into the bleachers, Melody's dad went for popcorn.

"Did you hear Mr. Bogey?" Howie asked his friends.

"He said he would get us if we didn't do our homework," Liza whined. "I want to go home and get started right now."

"Don't be silly," Eddie told her. "He's just trying to scare us."

"It's working," Liza said.

Howie pointed to the huge Bailey Bombers football team huddled in a circle on the field. "We should be scared. The bogeyman is after us."

"For snot's sake," Eddie said, taking his baseball cap and bopping Howie over the head. "Mr. Bogey is not the bogey-

man, and I'll prove it. Come on." Eddie jumped up and raced down the steps.

"Where is he going?" Melody asked.

"He's probably going to get into mischief," Liza said.

Howie shook his head. "We better keep him out of trouble."

"That's impossible with Eddie," Melody said. "Besides, the game is starting."

"We'll hurry," Howie said. The three kids hopped up and raced after Eddie. They saw him just as he ducked into the door marked PRIVATE.

"That's the locker room door," Liza said. "Eddie shouldn't go in there."

"We have to stop him before he gets in big trouble," Melody said. The three kids hurried through the door. It slammed shut behind them. They found themselves in total darkness.

"I can't see a thing," Liza whimpered.

"Listen," Howie told her. "I hear something."

"Ooooohhhhh!"

The kids heard a loud moaning sound.

"Ooooohhhhh!"

"What is that?" Melody asked.

"I don't know," Howie said, frantically trying to find the door handle behind him. "But whatever it is, it's getting closer!"

44

9

Ouch!

"Ouch!" Eddie said, snapping on the locker room lights.

"What's wrong with you?" Melody asked.

Eddie sat on the floor and rubbed his big toe. "I stubbed my toe," he complained.

Liza giggled. "You mean, that was you moaning?"

"I'm glad you think breaking my toe is funny," Eddie said. "Who did you think was moaning . . . the bogeyman?"

Instead of answering, Liza, Melody, and Howie looked around the locker room. "What are you looking for, anyway?" Howie asked.

"Proof that you're wrong about Mr. Bogey," Eddie told him.

45

"What kind of proof?" Melody asked.

Eddie limped over to a gray metal locker. "I'm not sure," he said. "But I'll know it when I see it." Eddie opened the locker and looked inside. "Nothing here but stinky socks," he said, slamming the locker shut.

"You should feel right at home," Melody said with a laugh.

Liza crossed her arms over her chest. "You shouldn't be looking in other people's stuff," she told Eddie.

"You want to find out if there really is a bogeyman, don't you?" Eddie asked.

"Well, sort of," Liza said slowly.

"Then this is where we need to look," Eddie said, stopping in front of a locker labeled B. BOGEY.

"Let me look in there," Melody said, jerking the locker handle.

"AHHHH!" Melody screamed as a huge figure tackled her to the ground. "Help!" she screamed. "Get it off me. It's the bogeyman!"

46

Eddie snatched the figure off Melody, and she rolled to safety. "Here's your bogeyman," Eddie said. He laughed and held up a black uniform. The football jersey had shoulder pads under it and a helmet resting on top.

"I thought you didn't believe in the bogeyman," Howie said to Melody.

"I don't," Melody lied. "But you have to admit having that uniform jump out at me was a little scary."

"Everything is fine," Liza said, helping Melody off the floor. "Howie has us scared with his talk of bogeymen and people getting us for not doing homework. We should get out of this creepy locker room and enjoy the game."

"Let's go," Eddie said as he headed for the door. But he never made it. A huge hand grabbed Eddie's shoulder.

10

Boogie-Woogie

Liza didn't wait to see what happened to Eddie. She took off running.

"AHHHH!" she screamed as she opened a door directly onto the playing field. She stumbled right into the middle of the Bailey Bombers cheerleaders. They were doing a cheer and shaking their black pom-poms.

"Get down, boogie-woogie-woogie!" the cheerleaders chanted. One cheerleader shook her pom-pom right in Liza's face.

By the time Liza found her way to her seat, her face looked like a cherry. People in the stands patted her on the back and asked her if she liked cheerleading. "I've never been so embarrassed," she said.

Melody, Howie, and Eddie sat down next to Liza. Melody put her arm around Liza and said, "Don't worry. No one will even remember it tomorrow."

"Why did you run?" Howie asked Liza. "Did you believe the bogeyman was going to get you?"

Liza gulped. "I didn't know what to think. I just got scared."

"The coach came in and told us we shouldn't be in the locker room. So we left," Melody explained.

"You mean Mr. Bogey didn't get you?" Liza asked Eddie.

"No," Eddie told her. "But he is about to get a touchdown." Eddie pointed to the football field. The game had started, and Mr. Bogey already had the ball. Everyone in the stands stood up and watched as Mr. Bogey ran. He ran and ran. The other team tried to catch him, but they couldn't get close. Mr. Bogey raced to the forty-yard line, then the thirty.

The cheerleaders started chanting, "Boogie-woogie, Bogey!"

When Mr. Bogey zipped to the twenty-yard line, someone behind Liza hollered, "Man, look at Bogey go!"

Someone else screamed, "Boogie-woogie, Bogey man!"

As Mr. Bogey crossed the five-yard line, the cheerleaders and the crowd yelled together, "Do the boogie-woogie, Bogey!"

When Mr. Bogey raced into the end zone for a touchdown, the crowd went bonkers. "Boogie-woogie!" the crowd roared.

"Did you see him?" Melody's father said, sitting down beside the kids with an armload of popcorn and sodas. "Have you ever seen anybody run like that?"

Howie took a bag of popcorn and a drink. "Thank you," he said to Melody's father. Howie passed a bag of popcorn to Eddie. "I have seen someone run like that," Howie whispered to Eddie.

"Where?" Eddie asked.

"In my nightmares," Howie said.

Eddie tossed a handful of popcorn at Howie. "Are you still whining about the bogeyman?" Eddie asked.

"I'm not the only one who thinks Mr. Bogey is the bogeyman," Howie told Eddie. "Just listen to the crowd."

The cheerleaders and the crowd clapped and cheered while Mr. Bogey did a little dance beside the goalpost. It was what the crowd chanted that made Eddie choke on a piece of popcorn.

"GET 'EM, BOGEYMAN! GET 'EM, BOGEYMAN!"

Howie looked at Eddie and nodded. "See," Howie told Eddie, "even the crowd knows. Our student teacher is the bogey-man!"

11

Hogwash

"I did it," Melody told her friends the next morning under the oak tree. "Or I guess I should say, I didn't do it."

"What are you talking about?" Eddie asked.

Melody looked around to be sure no one else was listening. "I didn't do my homework," Melody explained.

"So what?" Eddie asked. He couldn't understand why Melody was bragging. "I never do my homework."

Liza's eyes were big. "But Melody AL-WAYS does her homework!"

Melody grinned. "Not this time. I wanted to prove nothing would happen."

"So you proved Mr. Bogey isn't the bogeyman?" Liza asked.

"I knew it," Eddie said. "You proved Mr.

Bogey is just a windbag of a student teacher. Nothing bad happened."

"Well," Melody said, rubbing her eyes. "That's not exactly true. I didn't get a whole lot of sleep."

"Did you hear bumps under your bed?" Howie asked.

Melody shook her head. "No. I heard weird beeps."

"That sounds like an alien," Eddie said, "not the bogeyman."

"It was our smoke alarm," Melody explained. "It's in the living room underneath my bedroom. It needed a new battery."

Howie pointed a finger at Melody. "This is all because you didn't do your homework," he said. "Mr. Bogey got you by messing up the smoke alarm."

"I'm scared," Liza said. "Mr. Bogey is going to get us all. We're doomed!"

"You're safe as long as you did your homework," Howie explained.

Liza shivered and pulled her sweater

tight around her. "I don't want anything bad to happen to anyone. Isn't there some way to save ourselves?"

"I've been thinking about that," Howie said. "Everyone knows the bogeyman likes to scare people in the dark."

"So?" Melody asked.

"So, what if we all sleep with our lights on?" Howie suggested. "It might just get rid of the bogeyman."

"It wouldn't hurt to try," Melody agreed. "I'll tell Carey and Huey."

"But what about today?" Liza asked. "I'm scared."

"Don't worry," Melody said. "Mrs. Jeepers will be there the whole day. Mr. Bogey isn't going to get me or anybody else."

"That's where you're wrong," Howie said as the bell rang to start school. "Today is Mr. Bogey's day to teach all by himself. Mrs. Jeepers won't be there to save us!"

"You guys have been tackled one too

many times," Eddie said. "Since when do we need a vampire teacher to protect us from a student teacher?"

"Ever since we got the bogeyman for a student teacher," Howie told him. "You better be careful and watch what you do."

Eddie laughed before the kids went into the school building. "You watch what I do," Eddie said. "Because I'm going to prove once and for all that Mr. Bogey isn't the bogeyman!"

12

Unstoppable

Liza grabbed Howie. "What is he going to do?" she whimpered.

Howie looked like he'd just lost his best friend. "If I know Eddie," he said, "he's going to try and prove Mr. Bogey's just an ordinary teacher by doing what Eddie does best."

"By causing trouble," Melody finished.

"We have to stop him," Liza said. "Or the bogeyman will get him tonight."

"Never mind the bogeyman," Melody said. "If we don't stop Eddie, every teacher in Bailey City will get him!"

"When it comes to trouble," Howie said, "Eddie is unstoppable."

"We have to try," Melody said. "After all, he is our friend."

When Howie, Melody, and Liza

walked inside their third-grade room, they saw they were already too late. Eddie was busy doing what he did best.

Eddie flicked pencils off every desk he passed. When he reached the end of a row, he looked at the front of the room. Mr. Bogey hadn't seen a thing. He was too busy writing math problems on the board.

"If you practice these problems," Mr. Bogey said, "you will get a good grade on the math test tomorrow."

Eddie wasn't interested in math. He turned down another row and started pushing his classmates' papers to the floor.

"Quit that," Carey snapped. Then she waved her hand in the air. "Mr. Bogey," Carey called out, "Eddie's bothering me."

The rest of the class froze as Mr. Bogey slowly turned around and stared at Eddie. "I will keep my eye on Eddie until he finds his seat," Mr. Bogey growled.

Eddie wasn't scared. He closed his

eyes so he couldn't see a thing. Then he started waving his hands in front of him. "My desk," Eddie yelled. "I can't find it!"

Howie, Melody, and Liza stood in the doorway of their classroom. Melody held her breath and Liza closed her eyes. Howie looked like he was praying.

Mr. Bogey took one step, then another. His heavy footsteps thumped across the room in slow motion until he was right in front of Eddie.

Eddie opened his eyes. He had to look straight up to see Mr. Bogey's face.

"Sit down," Mr. Bogey growled. "Now."

When Eddie nodded and quickly found his chair, Melody started breathing again. "Maybe Eddie has learned his lesson," she whispered to Howie and Liza.

Howie nodded. "He shouldn't mess with the bogeyman."

The three friends hurried to their seats and started copying math problems. After solving each problem, Howie stole a glance at Eddie. It looked like Eddie had given up on his plan. Eddie's head was bent low over his desk so he could concentrate.

Howie was nearly finished with all the problems when a folded paper triangle slapped his cheek.

"First down," Eddie said out loud.

Howie looked up in time to see Eddie flick another paper football across the room. This one landed on top of Melody's head. "Field goal!" Eddie said with a grin before flicking another one halfway across the room. The third paper football landed right in the middle of Mr. Bogey's math book.

"Touchdown!" Eddie said. Then he stood up and did his own boogie-woogie touchdown dance.

"Sit down," Howie hissed. "Before the bogeyman gets you!"

But Howie's warning was too late. Mr. Bogey stomped across the room to flip off the light switch. The third-grade room went totally dark.

13

Bogey Is the Man

A chilly wind rattled the branches of the oak tree the next morning. Liza shivered and zipped up her jacket. "Do you think we'll ever see them again?" Liza said. Melody and Liza waited for their friends, but Eddie and Howie were very late.

Melody rolled her eyes. "If Mr. Bogey were really the bogeyman, he would've eaten Eddie yesterday."

"He didn't have a chance," Liza pointed out. "When he turned out the lights, Mrs. Jeepers came in the room."

Melody nodded. "That makes sense. Vampires like dark places."

"So Mr. Bogey had to wait until last night to get Eddie," Liza said. "Then he probably went to get Howie, too."

"No such luck," Melody said, pointing across the playground. Eddie and Howie were jogging toward them.

"What happened?" Liza asked. "Did the bogeyman get you?"

Eddie grinned. "No way," he said. "I slept like a baby."

"Of course you did," Howie said matter-of-factly.

"So you finally stopped believing in the bogeyman?" Melody asked Howie.

Howie shook a newspaper in front of his friends. "I don't believe the bogeyman lives in Bailey City anymore." Then Howie pointed to the newspaper headline.

"'Bob Bogey was the man,'" Liza, Melody, and Eddie read together.

Liza gasped. "It must be true! Even the newspaper said he's the bogeyman."

"No, it doesn't, booger brains," Eddie said. "You didn't read the rest of the article." He jabbed a finger at the paper. "It says Bogey was the man that led the

Bailey Bombers to victory — and into the professional league."

Howie nodded. "The Bailey Bombers left town last night," he said.

"What if he comes back?" Liza asked.

"He might come back," Eddie said, "but only if it's for the Bailey City Bogeyman Bowl game!"

"Does that mean Mr. Bogey isn't our student teacher anymore?" Liza asked.

Howie nodded. "He'll have to finish his student teaching somewhere else."

Eddie cheered and did his own boogie-woogie touchdown dance. "And that means we don't have to do our home-work!" he yelled.

Just then, the bell rang. "We still have to take the math test," Howie said.

Eddie stopped dancing. "What test?" he asked.

Liza rolled her eyes. "The test Mr. Bogey helped us practice for," she told Eddie.

Melody shook her finger at Eddie's

nose. "You were too busy causing trouble and didn't practice. So you're not ready for the test."

Liza giggled. "It looks like the bogeyman got Eddie after all!"

Debbie Dadey and Marcia Thornton Jones have fun writing stories together. When they both worked at an elementary school in Lexington, Kentucky, Debbie was the school librarian and Marcia was a teacher. During their lunch break in the school cafeteria, they came up with the idea of the Bailey School kids.

Recently Debbie and her family moved to Aurora, Illinois. Marcia and her husband still live in Kentucky where she continues to teach. How do these authors still write together? They talk on the phone and use computers and fax machines!

The Adventures of THE BAILEY SCHOOL KIDS ®

Creepy, weird, wacky and funny things happen to the Bailey School Kids!™ Collect and read them all!

SPENCER'S
adventures #5

Keeping tabs on a new pet snake is awfully hard work for Spencer. First, the hyper viper slips away and leads Spencer right into the smelly spray of a skunk! Then, while the class is baking a cake for the school carnival, Spencer suddenly realizes that his serpent is absent! Did his class make python pie?

Spencer's Adventures #5
Don't Bake That Snake!
by Gary Hogg

Look for these other *Spencer Adventures*:
#1: *Stop That Eyeball!*
#2: *Garbage Snooper Surprise*
#3: *Hair in the Air*
#4: *The Great Toilet Caper*

Slithering in a bookstore near you!